Charles H. Gardner

English History in Rhyme

Charles H. Gardner

English History in Rhyme

ISBN/EAN: 9783337271824

Printed in Europe, USA, Canada, Australia, Japan

Cover: Foto ©Andreas Hilbeck / pixelio.de

More available books at **www.hansebooks.com**

ENGLISH HISTORY

IN RHYME.

BY

MRS. CHARLES H. GARDNER,

PRINCIPAL OF SCHOOL FOR YOUNG LADIES,

603 FIFTH AVENUE,

NEW YORK CITY.

REVISED EDITION.

NEW YORK:

PUBLISHED BY THE AUTHOR.

1885.

Press of J. J. Little & Co.,
Nos. 10 to 20 Astor Place, New York.

PREFACE.

THIS Metrical Summary is one of a series, prepared, or in course of preparation, for use in schools, or for those who wish to memorize in a short time, and in an easy manner, the principal dates and events of history.

Its practical value has been tested in my own school, where I have used it in connection with a text-book. Pupils enjoy reciting it, and, when once learned, it is not readily forgotten.

The genealogical part of this second edition contains information not given elsewhere in any one book, and affords an answer to every question on the subject which would naturally arise.

The Scottish tables are unique, and are quite necessary in properly understanding many portions of the chronicles of England as well as of Scotland.

However skeptical some teachers may be, as to the mnemonic value of this method of study, all doubt will disappear upon a trial of its merits. A great point gained is that pupils take hold of the rhyme with enthusiasm, and do not realize while they are learning it that they are surmounting difficulties which have remained unconquered, except by those who have a phenomenal memory.

MARY RUSSELL GARDNER.

603 FIFTH AVENUE,
May, 1885.

ENGLISH HISTORY IN RHYME.

BRITISH AND ROMAN PERIOD (B.C. 55 TO A.D. 449).

From conquered Gaul, victorious Cæsar crossed the belt of sea, Julius Cæsar
To meet on Britain's fabled shore the swarming enemy.   55 B.C.
He made no lasting conquest, and a hundred years had fled,
Ere Claudius, in forty-three, another army led.   Claudius.
    43 A.D.
Suetonius, at Mona, laid the Druid altars low :
Agricola accomplished Southern Britain's overthrow.   Agricola.
   78 A.D.
In later times the Britons, by the Scots and Picts annoyed,
Besought the helping hand of Rome; her legions were em-
    ployed
In driving back invading Goths ; so, fair-haired Saxons came,
And kindred Angles found a home to which they gave a name.
To these untamed idolators by Gregory was sent
The monk Augustine, who declared the Christian faith in Kent.

SAXON PERIOD (449 TO 1066).

The Saxon Heptarchy comprised Northumbria, Mercia,
With Kent and Essex, Wessex, Sussex and East Anglia ;
By Egbert, in eight-twenty-seven, the parts were all com-   Egbert.
    bined.   827.
Then Ethelwolf and Ethelbald and Ethelbert we find,
With Ethelred ; and in the year eight hundred seventy-one
By good, sagacious Alfred, England's glory was begun.   Alfred.
   871.
In fierce encounter with the Dane, their blood-red flag went
    down,
And in administrative art, he won no less renown.

Edward.
901.
His son, the earliest Edward, came ; the valiant Athelstan,
And Edmund the Magnificent ; then Edred's rule began.
The death of Edwy's lovely wife was laid to Dunstan's charge:

Edgar.
958.
Eight tributary kings were found, to row King Edgar's barge.
Succeeding martyred Edward by Elfrida foully slain,
Was Second Ethelred, who fled the vengeful wrath of Sweyn.

Canute.
1016.
Brave Edmund Ironside divides his kingdom with Canute,
The Danish and Norwegian prince, of well-deserved repute.
His son, swift-running Harold, ruled, and then another Dane,
Hardicanute, the second son, who had a two-years' reign.

Edward the Confessor.
1042.
With Edward the Confessor came the Saxon line anew,
Regaining its supremacy, ten hundred forty-two.
An English noble followed, Harold Second, Godwin's son,

William I.
1066.
But by William, Duke of Normandy, was Albion claimed and
won.

NORMAN PERIOD (1066 TO 1154).

'Twas in ten hundred sixty-six, by Hastings Battle fought,
The stern and hated Norman rule to Anglia was brought.
The Conqueror, with ruthless hand, all insurrections quelled,
And gave his friends estates from which the Saxons were expelled.
The Feudal System soon became supreme throughout the land,
The "Curfew" tolled the evening hour ; the "Domesday Book" was planned.

When William died (ten-eighty-seven), both Normandy and Maine

William Rufus.
1087.
Were ceded to his eldest son ; in England was to reign
The younger, William Rufus—a severe, rapacious man ;
He conquered Scottish Malcolm ;—in his time Crusades began.

Henry I.
1100.
His brother Beauclerc followed, and by force of arms purloined

From careless Robert, Normandy, which was to England
    joined.
Prince William, Henry's son, was drowned; the sole inheritor
Was Maud, who married Henry Fifth, the German Emperor,
And afterwards, Plantagenet, the Earl of Anjou's son ;
But Stephen, at the king's demise, the sceptre seized upon.   Stephen.
    1135.
With lawlessness and civil war the country was astir ;
Matilda, fighting for the crown, took Stephen prisoner.
The latter, when restored, agreed the kingdom to award,
Upon his death, to Henry Second, eldest son of Maud.*

PLANTAGENET LINE (1154 TO 1485).

This first Plantagenet was heir to vast estates in France ;   Henry II.
    1154.
With Eleanor, his wife, he had her rich inheritance.
And when (eleven hundred fifty-four) all England is his own,
He tries to lift the burdens under which the people groan.
The Church and Baronage are brought in fealty to the state ;
Through stubborn opposition, proud À Becket meets his fate.
Hibernia, the " Isle of Saints." by Strongbow is subdued ;
And Scotland's " Lion William " yields a vassal's servitude.
In England, Gothic temples rise, and art and learning thrive,
But in the king's unhappy home rebellious children strive.

In eighty-nine, King Henry died ; his son, the " Lion Heart,"   Richard I.
    1189.
Succeeded, and in Third Crusade with Philip† bore a part.
On Moslem host of Saladin they dealt tremendous blows ;
But the Christian leaders quarrelled and became so bitter foes,
That Richard was by Leopold in Austria detained,
And, till ransomed by the English, in captivity remained.

His craven brother, Lackland, disregarded Arthur's claim,   John.
    1199.
And, conniving at his murder, was received with scorn and
    shame.

---

* Maud or Matilda.   † Philip Augustus of France.

As Philip's vassal, wicked John was summoned to explain,
But, failing to obey the call, lost all his French domain.
Pope Innocent compelled the king to bow to his decree,
And "Magna Charta" guarded well the people's liberty.

nry III In twelve-sixteen, comes Henry Third, pacific and humane ;—
1216.
The kingdom suffers great distress in this protracted reign.
For storms of civil discord rage, in council hall confer
The mailéd barons ; Lewes * fought, the king is prisoner.
De Montfort calls a parliament, with knights from every shire,
The delegates from cities and from boroughs first appear.
And thus the House of Commons rose. Prince Edward's
trusty sword,
At Evesham, overthrew the Earl and Henry's power re-
stored.

ward I This bold Crusader Edward, came, twelve hundred seventy-
1272.
two ;
He conquered Wales, and Scotland's might determined to
subdue.
The ruler, Alexander Third, had left no heirs direct ;
So, one of two competitors King Edward must elect,—
John Baliol, or Robert Bruce :—the former was preferred ;
But Edward grew so arrogant, that Scottish pride was stirred.
The standard of revolt was raised, the king his wrath made
known ;
He took the crown from Baliol,—removed the "Chair of
Scone."
Avenging William Wallace fled from scattered hearth-stone
fires,
And summoned all the clans to guard the birthright of their
sires.

---

* Pron. Lew'es.

"The Bruce" was hunted like a deer through fen and forest
    wide,
Till Edward, weary with the chase, and breathing vengeance,
    died.

The stern and warlike father left a weak, unworthy child—   Edward II.
A dissipated trifler, by his favorites beguiled.   1307.
The Scots, inspired by Robert Bruce, triumphant in their turn,
Put England's chivalry to flight, on field of Bannockburn.
This victory, to Scotland her enfranchisement secured ;
But greater shame and misery the hapless king endured ;
For factious nobles, Mortimer and Edward's guilty wife,
Most cruelly deprived him of authority and life.

In thirteen hundred twenty-seven, succeeded Edward Third ; EdwardIII.
Base Mortimer and Isabelle due punishment incurred.   1327.
Young David wore the Scottish crown his father Robert won ;
But Edward chose as vassal king the former Baliol's son,
Repulsed the Scots at Halidon Hill ; compelled their king to
    flee ;
Proclaimed himself the heir to France ;—was victor at Crecy.
'Twas there the Black Prince won his spurs : the English
    took Calais ;
Defeated Scots at Neville's Cross, and French at Poitiers.
Great Edward Third reigned fifty years ; was able, just and
    wise ;
Gave England new commercial strength, by active enterprise.
To us, this literary age has left how rich a dower,
In Wickliffe and in Mandeville, in Chaucer and in Gower.

Prince Edward's son, the second Richard, peacefully succeeds: Richard II.
Increased taxation for the wars wide disaffection breeds ;   1377.
Watt Tyler led a rebel mob, which speedily was quelled,
And Henry, son of John of Gaunt, to foreign lands expelled,

Returned in arms, and malcontents so gently he bespoke,
The king, forsaken and deposed, gave way to Bolingbroke.

HOUSE OF LANCASTER (1399 TO 1461).

Henry IV.
1399.
In thirteen hundred ninety-nine, this crafty Henry came,
But Lionel's great-grandson had a higher legal claim.
The Percies, Earl of Douglas and Glendower, all combined,
To youthful Edmund Mortimer the regal right assigned.
With meagre force at Shrewsbury, rash Hotspur ventured all,
Foreseeing not the tragic fate which swiftly did befall.

Henry V.
1413.
In fourteen-thirteen, jovial Hal, of riotous renown,
Cast off his old associates, as he put on the crown :
Reviving England's claim to France, in shining armor dight,
On far-famed field of Agincourt, he won a glorious fight.
Then married Catherine of France ; as Regent, took the lead :
'Twas said, when Charles the Sixth should die, King Henry
    should succeed.
In fourteen hundred twenty-two, both Charles and Henry
    died ;
Henry VI.
1422.
Young Henry Sixth was then enthroned, the Dauphin set
    aside.
The war rekindled, Joan of Arc, by spirit-voices led,
To save her country, sought the field, where brave com-
    patriots bled.
The siege of Orleans was raised, and Charles,* at Rheims was
    crowned,
But, shame to France ! the high-souled maid a fiery death-
    bed found.

The wife of timid Henry Sixth was Margaret of Anjou,
As spirited and merciless as he was meek and true ;

---

* Charles VII. of France.

The death of noble Gloucester,* and the loss of French es-
tates,
With Henry's incapacity, such discontent creates,
That able Richard, Duke of York, Protector of the realm,
Asserted his ancestral right to govern at the helm :
And thus commenced a civil war which lasted thirty years ;   Wars of the
Destroyed the old nobility, and drenched the land with tears.   Roses.
'Twas called the War of Roses, for the Yorkists wore the   1455-1485.
white :
The reigning house of Lancaster with red ones was bedight.

At St. Albans and Northampton, Henry's force was put to
rout ;
While, at sanguinary Wakefield, fortune's wheel was turned
about ;
The vanquished Duke of York was killed, but Edward   Edward IV.
Fourth, his son,   1461.
Soon afterwards became the king, in fourteen sixty-one.
Lancastrians still resisted, but by Towton's bloody field,   House of
And other sad reverses, their unhappy lot was sealed.   York.
Then Warwick changed to Henry's side and he was rein-   1461-1485.
stalled ;
The Earl, at Barnet overthrown, King Edward was recalled.
At Tewkesbury, Margaret and her son fought bravely, but in
vain ;
The queen was taken to the Tower,—the young Prince Ed-
ward slain.
At Henry's death, Lancastrians relinquished every hope,
And Edward, firmly seated, gave his vices fullest scope :
He doomed his brother Clarence, died in fourteen eighty-
three.
The earliest English printed book in Edward's reign we see.

---

* Pron. Gloster.

Then came the little princes, basely smothered in the Tower
By their wicked uncle, Gloucester, who usurped the royal
power.

Richard III. King Richard's triumph was but short :—in fourteen eighty-
1483. five,
He rode, all crowned, to Bosworth Field, but ne'er came off
alive.

Henry VII. " Long live King Henry ! " was the shout which signalized his
1485. fate,
And which the haughty Tudor rule did thus inaugurate.

The Tudors. Although Elizabeth of York became the monarch's wife,
1485–1603. Suspicion of the rival house embittered all his life.
As Edward's * nephew Simnel posed ; and Warbeck, as his
son.
The " Yorkist Rose " (poor Warwick !) plucked, of white ones
there were none.
This avaricious Henry reigned till fifteen hundred nine.
The usages of feudal times were then on the decline ;
It was an age of great events :—America was found ;
. The Turks set foot in Europe ; ancient learning spread
around ;
The use of firearms changed the form of battle's stern array ;
The art of printing ushered in a new and glorious day.

Henry VIII. The " Bluff King Hal," of martial fame so emulous and vain,
1509. Joined hands with Venice, Leo Tenth, and Ferdinand of
Spain,
Against King Louis Twelfth of France.   James Fourth, on
Flodden Field,
With flower of Scotch nobility, his soul to God did yield.

---

* Edward IV.

When Francis First and Charles the Fifth high potentates be-
came,
Each one desired upon his side inconstant Henry's name.
The king, on " Field of Cloth of Gold," to Francis seemed a
friend ;
But Charles, by courting Wolsey, tried to gain his selfish end.
As stout " Defender of the Faith " the monarch now appears,
And of his right to Catherine has pious doubts and fears.
For charming Mistress Boleyn,* Henry quarrels with the Pope,
And Wolsey, humbled and disgraced, renounces earthly hope.
Though England with the Church of Rome dissevers every
tie,
This " Glorious Reformation " brings no real liberty.
The despot makes an end of all who dare to cross his path ;
Poor Anne, with More and Surrey, falls the victim of his
wrath.
Jane Seymour, homely Anne of Cleves, Kate Howard, Cath-
erine Parr,
Of this " Blue Beard " in royal guise successive consorts are.

In fifteen hundred forty-seven, the little son was crowned— Edward VI.
Good Edward Sixth, for gentleness and piety renowned. 1547.
His uncle, Somerset, controlled with almost kingly power,
But, being charged with treason, was beheaded in the Tower.
Northumberland, who followed, gave in marriage to his son
The Lady Grey, and for her rights became the champion.
For her, the passive Edward set his sister's claims aside ;
And when in fifteen fifty-three, the feeble monarch died,
His modest Cousin Jane was urged to take the vacant throne,
But Catherine's daughter, Mary, seized upon it as her own. Mary.
Proclaimed the Queen, she sent her foes to prison or the block, 1553.
And soon to Holy See of Rome restored her wandering flock :

---

* Pron Bullen.

With Rogers, Ridley, Latimer, who perished at the stake,
The contrite Cranmer suffered for his dear religion's sake.
The Queen's detested husband, Philip Second, King of Spain,
A war with France, by Mary's help, was able to maintain ;
They gained St. Quentin's, but, alas ! they lost belov'd Calais,
Which had been held by Englishmen since great King Edward's day.

Ere long, neglected Mary died, in fifteen fifty-eight ;
Elizabeth. Elizabeth, the Virgin Queen, was then enthroned in state.
1558. She brought the Church of England back,—made every one
conform.
With his Armada, Philip sought the British Isle to storm.
Brave Raleigh, Drake and Frobisher sailed o'er the Western
Sea,
And Shakespeare, Spenser, Bacon formed a brilliant galaxy.
The lovely heir of James the Fifth, fair Mary, Queen of Scots,
Was sentenced to a cruel fate for treasonable plots.
The Queen assisted Henry Fourth against the Spanish might,
And condemned the wayward Essex as a false and recreant
knight ;
His tragic death so wrought upon her tenderness and pride,
That she, in sixteen hundred three, in bitter anguish died.

STUART PERIOD (1603–1714).

James I. The Tudors ended, James the Sixth, the last of Scotland's
1603. kings
To England called, as James the First, the House of Stuart
brings.
This son of Mary, Queen of Scots, ill-mannered, but well-read,
" The wisest fool in Europe " was, as Sully aptly said.
His doctrine of authority by a divine decree,
With English views of liberty did not at all agree.

His cousin, Arabella, was proposed to take his place,
And Raleigh, for complicity, was brought to deep disgrace.
Guy Fawkes's match did not go off, his head went off instead,
And king and Parliament were saved from consequences
 dread.
Some colonists in sixteen seven, at Jamestown anchor cast,
And Puritans to Plymouth went, despite the wintry blast.
The Bible was translated by the fifty chosen men.
James died in sixteen twenty-five, and Charles succeeded then.

The folly of the father was transmitted to the son ;   Charles I.
And "right divine to govern wrong" was still insisted on.   1625.
So, when the Parliament refused to grant the king's demands,
He used most arbitrary means to carry out his plans.
He forced on Scots and Puritans the English liturgy :
The former signed their Covenant ;—the latter crossed the sea.
Long Parliament was then convoked, and Strafford, Laud im-
 peached ;
To civil war, in forty-two, the grievous quarrel reached.   Civil War.
For six long years the contests rage, and Cromwell fiercely   1642–48.
 guides
To victory, at Marston Moor, his famous Ironsides.
In vain Prince Rupert and the King at Naseby hotly fought :
And when, with Scots, the fugitive a safe asylum sought,
They sold him to the Parliament. By "Pride's Purge" this
 was cleared
Of Presbyterian members : so, derided "Rump" appeared :
The fifty Independents rule, their fallen king arraign,
Decree his death, and with his blood their country's annals
 stain.

In sixteen hundred forty-nine, the Commonwealth arose :   Cromwell.
As Lord Protector, Cromwell ruled, and silenced all his foes ;   1649.

Rebellious Ireland was subdued ; at Dunbar, Scots were beat ;
And young Prince Charles, by them proclaimed, at Worces-
ter * met defeat.
He fled and wandered in disguise ; one day, the Royal Oak
Concealed him from the searching eyes of the pursuing folk.
Upon the sea, by Blake's success, proud England rode as
queen,
And not Van Tromp's defiant broom could sweep the Channel
clean.
Though Cromwell raised his country's fame to so exalted
state,
Renewed conspiracies and plots revealed the common hate.
He dies in sixteen fifty-eight : his eldest son succeeds,
But abdicates in fifty-nine, and Monk the army leads ;
Unites contending factions, and a Parliament is called :
The " Restoration " follows ; Charles the Second is installed.

Charles II. 1660. This merry, lazy, vicious king is well described as one
" Who never foolish thing had said, nor ever wise one done."
The too exultant people found their confidence abused ;
The prodigal, to feed his purse, the meanest measures used,—
As selling Dunkirk. With the Dutch was waged, at his com-
mand,
A war, in which the Duke of York obtained New Netherland.
The " Dreadful Plague," the " London Fire " spread terror
far and wide ;
De Ruyter's ships sailed up the Thames and humbled Eng-
land's pride.
When Clarendon was banished, came the bold Cabal's in-
trigue :
To thwart ambitious Louis'† schemes was formed the " Triple
League."

---

* Pron. Wooster.   † Louis XIV. of France.

The " Habeas Corpus Act" was passed ; the " Rye House
    Plot" devised :
Charles died in sixteen eighty-five ; to James the throne de-
    mised.
In Charles's time were Bunyan, Boyle, and Locke, and New-
    ton wise ;
And Milton, groping in the dark, discovered Paradise.

Of James, the claimant Monmouth, begged the life that   James II.
    Sedgemoor spared,   1685.
While "Lambs of Kirke" and "Tiger Jeffreys" feasts of
    blood prepared.
The king displeased the populace by giving Papists power,
And the bishops for rebellion were imprisoned in the Tower.
The keen-eyed Prince of Orange, who was James's son-in-law,
In all the spreading discontent his own advantage saw.
Invited by the English, William landed at Torbay ;
And James, deserted by his friends, stole hurriedly away.

This "Glorious Revolution" was in sixteen eighty-eight ;   William and
According to the " Bill of Rights" must William rule the state.   . Mary.
The banished king, with Louis'* aid, returned to push his   1688.
    cause,
And first aroused the Irish, who received him with applause.
He lost the "Battle of the Boyne," and fled to France again :
The Scotch and Irish were dispersed, the Glencoe clan was
    slain.
The naval battle of La Hogue decided James's fate ;
But not till Peace of Ryswick did the French war terminate.
Till seventeen two, King William ruled, a brave, sagacious
    man ;
Then James's second daughter came,—the heavy, good Queen
    Anne.

---

* Louis XIV. of France.

2

Anne.
1702.

The long "Succession War," which filled this memorable
reign,
Secured to Louis' grandson the disputed crown of Spain.
Great genius did the Prince Eugene and Marlborough dis-
play,
At Ramillies and Oudenarde, Blenheim and Malplaquet.
Gibraltar's frowning fortress fell, by British sailors won ;
The "Peace of Utrecht" made with France, announced the
contest done.
'Twas framed in seventeen thirteen, and the queen soon after
died ;
To this, the name "Augustan Age " has ever been applied.
Swift, Addison, and Steele and Pope adorned their brilliant
time,
With stinging wit, and pungent thought, and cultivated rhyme.

HOUSE OF BRUNSWICK (1714).

In reign of Anne, the act was passed, which Scotland closely
bound
To England, with one parliament ; and, at her death, was
crowned

George I.
1714.

The stolid George of Hanover, who true succession claims,
As being by the younger branch the great-grandson of
James.
The Chevalier St. George appeared to lead the Jacobites,
And beacons burned, and pibrochs shrilled, on Scotland's
craggy heights.
But, though the Highlanders were roused, the English barely
stirred,
While those who favored James's cause sore punishment in-
curred.
Discomfited, he fled to France, which pledged itself to peace.
In twenty-seven, from German George the English had release.

The son, a little, hasty man, inherited the throne ; George II.
1727.
But Caroline, his brilliant wife, with greater splendor shone.
Though Walpole's counsel was for peace, George Second took
    the field,
When wronged Theresa, Austria's Queen, to him her cause War of the
Austrian
Succession.
1740-1748.
    appealed.
The valiant king won Dettingen, but Cumberland, his son,
By Marshal Saxe, at Fontenoy, was signally outdone.
Charles Edward, Young Pretender, came to press his father's
    right,
And moving south from Preston Pans, filled London with af-
    fright.
The battle of Culloden was the last on British soil,
And, after it, the Stuarts ceased the country to embroil.
The Treaty of Aix-la-Chapelle, in seventeen forty-eight,
Confirmed to proud Theresa her imperial estate.
In Seven Years' War, with Prussian Frederick England stood Sev'n Years
War.
1756-1763.
    allièd,
And Pitt, the mighty Commoner, the power of France defied.
Her rule in North America received a deadly blow,
And Robert Clive, in India, laid French ambition low.
The splendid Plassy victory and Pondicherry's fall
To English rule surrendered the Carnatic and Bengal.

In seventeen sixty, Farmer George, a dull, but kindly man, George III
1760-1820.
His reign of sixty fruitful years auspiciously began.
In sixty-three, by Paris Peace the Seven Years' War was closed,
And on her well-earned laurels England thankfully reposed.
But her restrictive policy in all colonial trade,
And the taxes in America which she unjustly laid,
Provoked another seven years' war : in seventeen eighty-
    three
Th' United States from British rule became entirely free.

In seventeen eighty-nine, broke out the great revolt in France:
All Europe joined to hold in check its wild extravagance.
And when Poor Louis was no more, and Bonapârte aspired
To universal sovereignty, the English heart was fired.
Though younger William Pitt controlled, affairs went ill on
    land ;
But England's mighty men-of-war no rival could withstand.
Trafalgar and the Nile were won : the first cost Nelson's life ;
And, while the continental powers fell helpless in the strife,
Undaunted England stood alone, protected by the sea,
And was, throughout Napoleon's reign, his bitter enemy.
At last, in eighteen fifteen, the disturber of the world,
By Wellington, at Waterloo, was from his empire hurled.

While England's peace by foreign foes so grievously was vexed,
Unruly Ireland, overpowered, to England was annexed.
In eighteen twenty died the king,—deaf, sightless and insane ;

George IV. His son, the Regent, George the Fourth, began a troubled
1820–1830.   reign.
The " Nation's Darling," Charlotte, died: to Caroline's defence
Lord Brougham woke the people, by his fervid eloquence.
The English helped the Greeks throw off the heavy Turkish
    yoke,
And Navarino's victory the slavish thraldom broke.
O'Connel and Sir Robert Peel relieved the Catholics
From laws restrictive, which forbade their share in politics.

William IV. In eighteen thirty, William Fourth, another son, succeeds ;
1830–1837. The need of change in franchise law my Lord John Russell
    pleads.
A bill is passed, by which the right of voting is to lie
More widely with the middle class, and portioned equally.
Throughout the British colonies the slaves are all set free.
In eighteen thirty-seven, is raised to regal dignity

Victoria, the only child of Edward, Duke of Kent :
She could not rule in Hanover, which to her uncle went.
The union of the Canadas was ultimately sealed ;
Through zeal of Cobden and of Bright, the Corn Laws were
    repealed.
The Chartists clamored for reform ; the hated opium trade
Was forced by war on China, and the Nankin Treaty made.
The English, threatened at Cabul, soon left Afghanistan ;
Defeating Sikhs, they gained control o'er all of Hindostan.
The French and English draw the sword in eighteen fifty-four,
To make the Russian Nicholas his Turkish spoils restore.
Against mail-clad Sebastopol a weary siege is laid ;
Through Balaklava's valley sweeps the fated Light Brigade ;
The fortress Malakoff is stormed, in eighteen fifty-six ;
To Paris Peace the warring powers their signatures affix.

In India, in fifty-nine, rebellion raised its head,
And Méerut, Delhi, Cawnpore, Nana's fiendish hordes o'er-
    spread.
At Lucknow, Campbell's Highlanders saved Havelock's feeble
    band,
And Sepoy mutineers were crushed, through all the troubled
    land.
The old East India Company then laid its sceptre down,
And the guidance of the Empire was surrendered to the crown.

To white-winged ships of commerce China's ports were open
    thrown ;
Japan, through Elgin's influence, gave entrance to her own.
In Magdala, the British, bound in rock-based citadel,
Were free once more, when Theodore, the wild usurper, fell.
A brilliant, brief Ashantee war gives Wolseley early fame :
The English and the Muscovite, Shere Ali's favors claim.

1878. The former twice invade Cabul to gain a safe frontier,
And keep in check the only foe that they have cause to fear.
Zulu War. The Zulus in South Africa, attack the colonists,
1879. But all their savage fury Wolseley gallantly resists.
War in On Tel-el-Kebir's battle-ground he captures Arabi.
Egypt. In the Soudan, El Mahdi holds supreme ascendency.
Conservatives and Liberals, in turn, have been in power :
A Gladstone and a Beaconsfield have had their triumph hour.
Though Albert died in '61, Victoria lives to reign,
And wields a wise, impartial sway o'er all her vast domain.

SCOTTISH GENEALOGY.—NO. 1. KINGS OF SCOTLAND.

Kenneth Mac Alpin (836-59). First King of all Scotland.

Donald III. (859-61).

Constantine II. (863-81).

Donald IV. (893-904).

Malcolm I. (943-53).

Grig, rebel chieftain, called Gregory the Great, usurped the throne 882, and was expelled 893.

Hugh (881-82).

Constantine III. (904-43).

Induff (953-61).

Culen, Prince of Cumberland (965-70).

Duff (961-65).

Kenneth III. (970-94).

Kenneth IV. (994-1003), slain by Malcolm II.

Malcolm II. (1003-1033), Regulus or Prince of Cumberland.

Constantine IV., d. 995, reigned only a few months.

Beatrix.

Daoda.

Bodhe, slain with his father.

Crynin, Abbot of Dunkeld.

Finley, Thane of Ross. Slain 1020.

Macbeth Finley (1040-56).

Gruoch.

Gruoch (Lady Macbeth). Macbeth Maormor of Ross.

Kilcomgain, Thane of Moray.

Duncan (1033-40). d. Siward, Prince of Northumberland.

Malcolm III., Canmore or Great Head (1057-93).

Margaret, sister of Edgar Atheling.

Donald Bane (1093-97). With him the Gaelic or Celtic Period ends.

Lulach.

Margaret. Edgar Atheling.

Note 1.—The Scots did not adhere to the usual order of succession, but generally preferred the brother, to the son of the last king.

Note 2.—The northern districts of Scotland were ruled by powerful chiefs called Maormors.

Note 3.—Macbeth was not a usurper, but the natural supporter of the claims of his wife, and Lulach, her son by a former marriage. Lady Macbeth had deadly injuries to avenge on the reigning monarch. Her grandfather had been dethroned and slain by Malcolm, her brother assassinated, and her first husband burned in his castle. She sought refuge in the district of Ross, and gave her hand to Macbeth. Macbeth's father had been slain by Duncan, so, instigated by ambition and revenge, he attacked and slew Duncan at a place called Bothgowan, near Elgin. Macbeth immediately mounted the throne, and his reign was one of great prosperity. He and his wife were benefactors of the Church and the poor.

SCOTTISH GENEALOGY.—NO. 2. SCOTO-SAXON PERIOD.

Malcolm III. (1057-93).

Ingebiorg, widow of Earl Thorfin of Orkney.

Margaret, sister of Edgar Atheling.

Duncan II., 1095 d. Reigned only a few months. Murdered by Donald Bane.

Eadward, slain with his father, in battle.

Eadmund, died a penitent in a monastery.

Eadgar, 1097-1107.

Alexander (1107-24). Sibilla, d. Henry I. of England.

David (1124-53). Matilda d. Waltheof, Earl of Northumberland.

Eadgyth or Maud. Henry I. of England.

Mary. Eustace, Count of Boulogne.

Matilda. Stephen, King of England.

Henry, Prince of Scotland, and Earl of Huntingdon, d. 1152.
Ada, d. Earl of Warrenne and Surrey.

Malcolm IV. (1153-65).

William the Lion (1165-1214). Ermengarde de Beaumont.

Ada. Floris III., Count of Holland. Their descendant, Floris V., was competitor with Bruce and Baliol.

David, Earl of Huntingdon.

Alexander II. (1214-49).

Joan, d. John, King of E.

Mary, d. Ingelram de Courcy.

Alexander III. (1249-86).

Margaret, d. Henry III., King of E. | Joletta, d. Robert, Count de Dreux.

Margaret (d. 1283).
Eric, King of Norway.

Margaret, the Maid of Norway (1286-90).
The last descendant of William the Lion ; heir to the throne at the age of three ; died on the voyage from Norway to Scotland.

SCOTTISH GENEALOGY.—NO. 3.

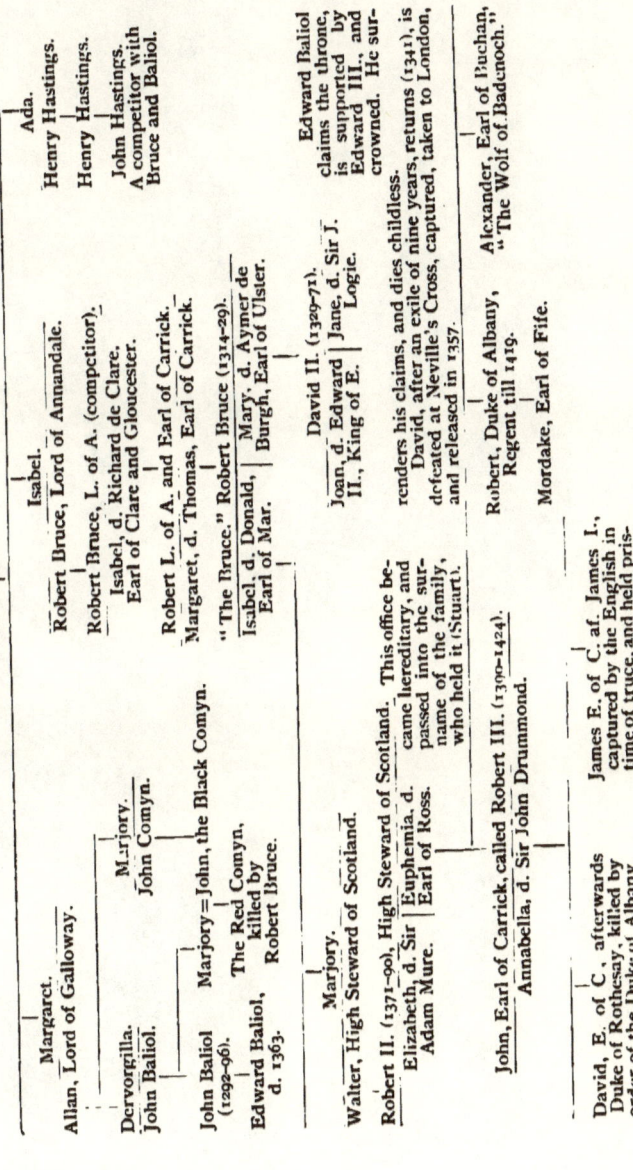

David, Earl of Huntingdon.
Maud, d. Hugh of Chester.

Margaret.
Allan, Lord of Galloway.

Dervorgilla.
John Baliol.

Marjory.
John Comyn.

John Baliol
(1292-96).

Marjory=John, the Black Comyn.

The Red Comyn,
killed by
Robert Bruce.

Edward Baliol,
d. 1363.

Marjory.
Walter, High Steward of Scotland.

Robert II. (1371-90), High Steward of Scotland. This office became hereditary, and
passed into the sur-
name of the family,
who held it (Stuart).

Elizabeth, d. Sir
Adam Mure.

Euphemia, d.
Earl of Ross.

John, Earl of Carrick, called Robert III. (1390-1424).
Annabella, d. Sir John Drummond.

David, E. of C., afterwards
Duke of Rothesay, killed by
order of the Duke of Albany.

James E. of C. af. James I.,
captured by the English in
time of truce, and held prisoner by Henry IV. till 1424

Isabel.
Robert Bruce, Lord of Annandale.

Robert Bruce, L. of A. (competitor).

Isabel, d. Richard de Clare,
Earl of Clare and Gloucester.

Robert L. of A. and Earl of Carrick.
Margaret, d. Thomas, Earl of Carrick.

"The Bruce." Robert Bruce (1314-29).

Isabel, d. Donald,
Earl of Mar.

Mary, d. Aymer de
Burgh, Earl of Ulster.

David II. (1329-71).
Joan, d. Edward
II., King of E.

Jane, d. Sir J.
Logie.

renders his claims, and dies childless.
David, after an exile of nine years, returns (1341), is
defeated at Neville's Cross, captured, taken to London,
and released in 1357.

Robert, Duke of Albany,
Regent till 1419.

Mordake, Earl of Fife.

Alexander, Earl of Buchan,
"The Wolf of Badenoch."

Ada.
Henry Hastings.
Henry Hastings.
John Hastings.
A competitor with
Bruce and Baliol.

Edward Baliol
claims the throne,
is supported by
Edward III., and
crowned. He sur-

SCOTTISH GENEALOGY.—NO. 4.

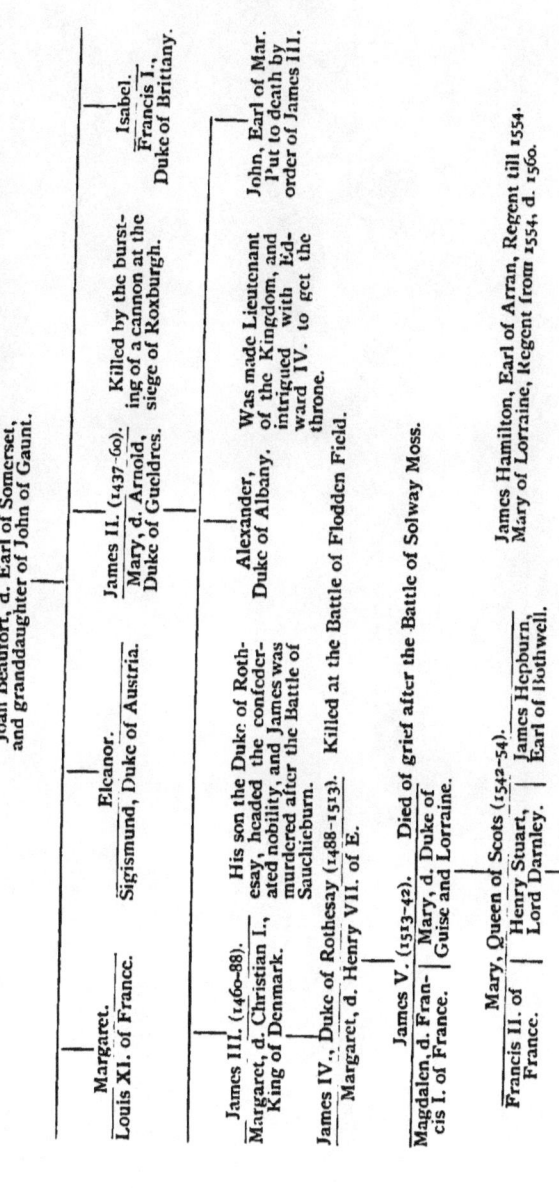

James I. (1424-37).
Joan Beaufort, d. Earl of Somerset, and granddaughter of John of Gaunt.

Assassinated by his nobles.

Margaret.
Louis XI. of France.

Eleanor.
Sigismund, Duke of Austria.

James II. (1437-60).
Mary, d. Arnold, Duke of Gueldres.

Killed by the bursting of a cannon at the siege of Roxburgh.

Isabel.
Francis I., Duke of Brittany.

James III. (1460-88).
Margaret, d. Christian I., King of Denmark.

His son the Duke of Rothesay, headed the confederated nobility, and James was murdered after the Battle of Sauchieburn.

Alexander, Duke of Albany.

Was made Lieutenant of the Kingdom, and intrigued with Edward IV. to get the throne.

John, Earl of Mar.
Put to death by order of James III.

James IV., Duke of Rothesay (1488-1513).
Margaret, d. Henry VII. of E.

Killed at the Battle of Flodden Field.

James V. (1513-42).
Magdalen, d. Francis I. of France. | Mary, d. Duke of Guise and Lorraine.

Died of grief after the Battle of Solway Moss.

Mary, Queen of Scots (1542-54).
Francis II. of France. | Henry Stuart, Lord Darnley. | James Hepburn, Earl of Bothwell.

James Hamilton, Earl of Arran, Regent till 1554.
Mary of Lorraine, Regent from 1554, d. 1560.

James VI. (1567-1625).
Afterwards James I. of England.

ENGLISH GENEALOGY.—NO. 1.—KINGS OF ENGLAND.

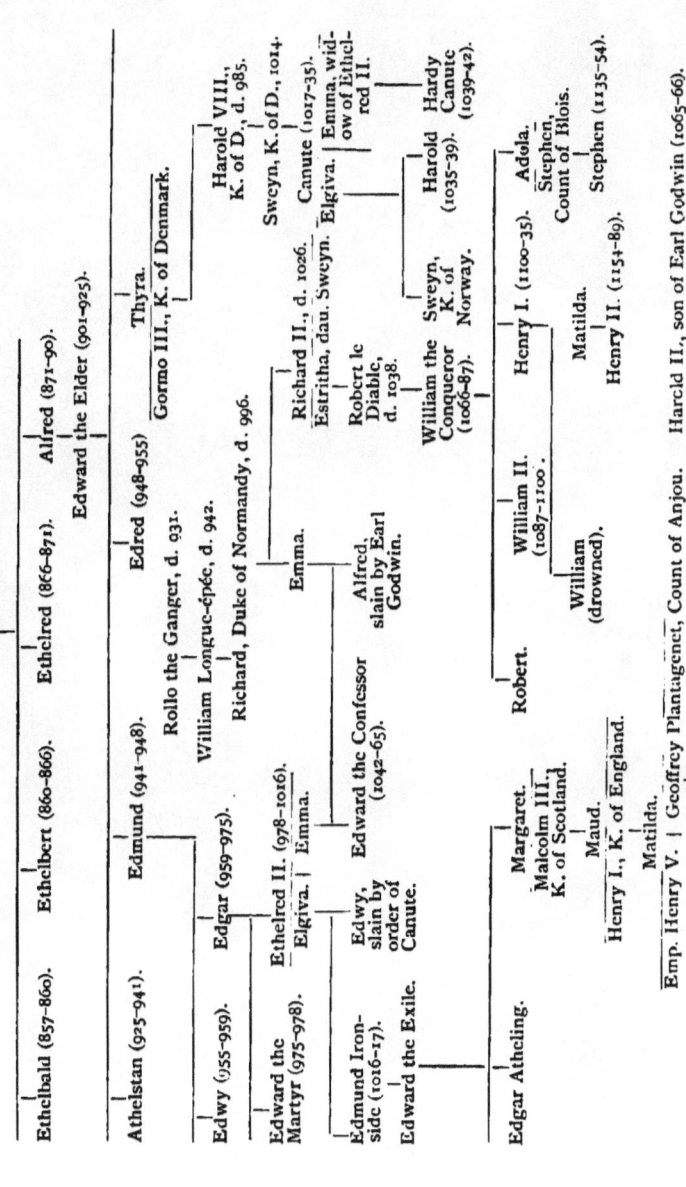

ENGLISH GENEALOGY.—NO. 2.—THE HOUSE OF PLANTAGENET.

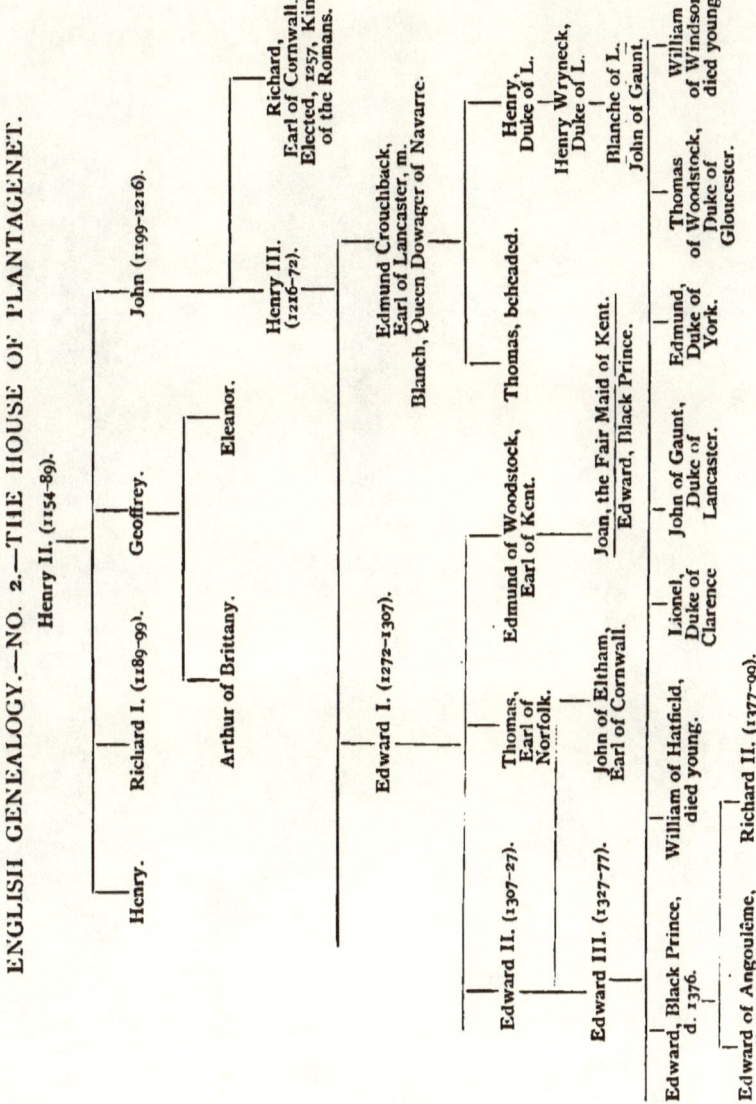

Henry II. (1154–89).

Henry.

Richard I. (1189–99).

Geoffrey.
— Arthur of Brittany.
— Eleanor.

John (1199–1216).
— Richard, Earl of Cornwall. Elected, 1257, King of the Romans.
— Henry III. (1216–72).

Henry III. (1216–72).
— Edward I. (1272–1307).
— Edmund Crouchback, Earl of Lancaster, m. Blanch, Queen Dowager of Navarre.
  — Thomas, beheaded.
  — Henry, Duke of L.
    — Henry Wryneck, Duke of L.
    — Blanche of L. = John of Gaunt.

Edward I. (1272–1307).
— Edward II. (1307–27).
— Thomas, Earl of Norfolk.
— Edmund of Woodstock, Earl of Kent.
  — Joan, the Fair Maid of Kent. = Edward, Black Prince.

Edward II. (1307–27).
— Edward III. (1327–77).

Edward III. (1327–77).
— Edward, Black Prince, d. 1376.
  — Edward of Angoulême, died young.
  — Richard II. (1377–99).
— William of Hatfield, died young.
— Lionel, Duke of Clarence.
— John of Gaunt, Duke of Lancaster.
— Edmund, Duke of York.
— Thomas of Woodstock, Duke of Gloucester.
— William of Windsor, died young.

John of Eltham, Earl of Cornwall.

ENGLISH GENEALOGY.—NO. 3.—THE HOUSE OF PLANTAGENET.

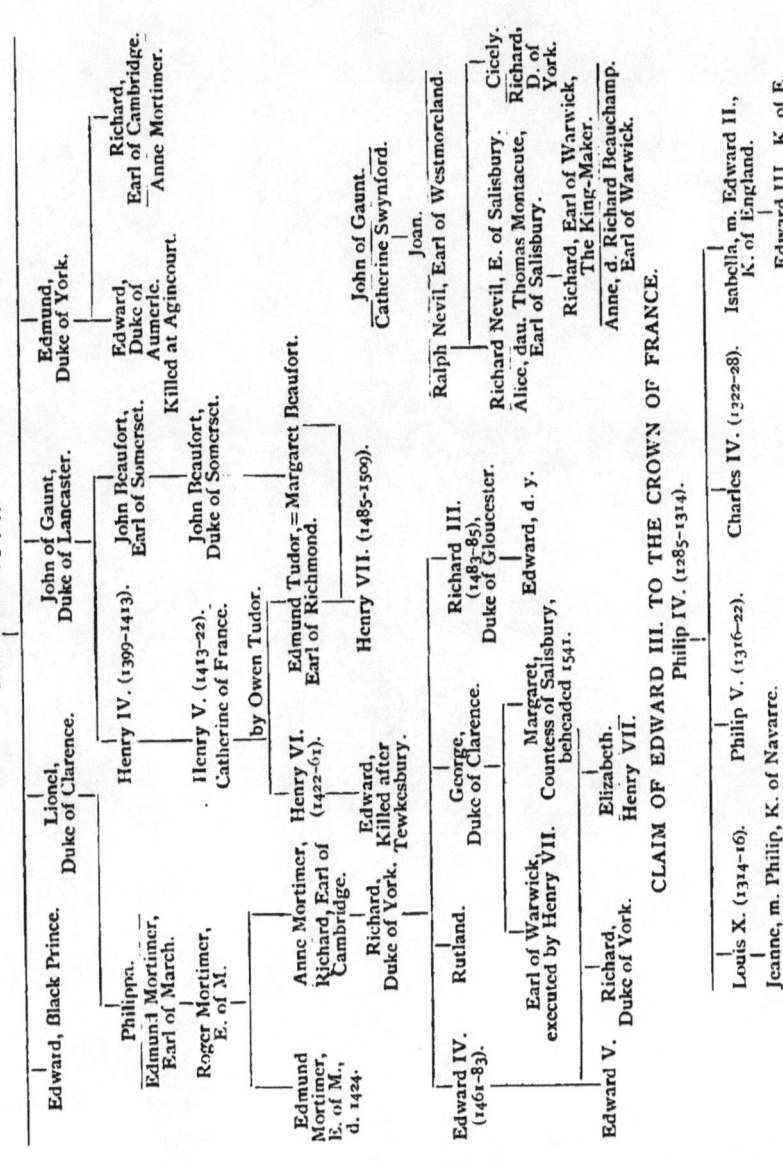

ENGLISH GENEALOGY.—NO. 4.—THE HOUSES OF TUDOR AND STUART.

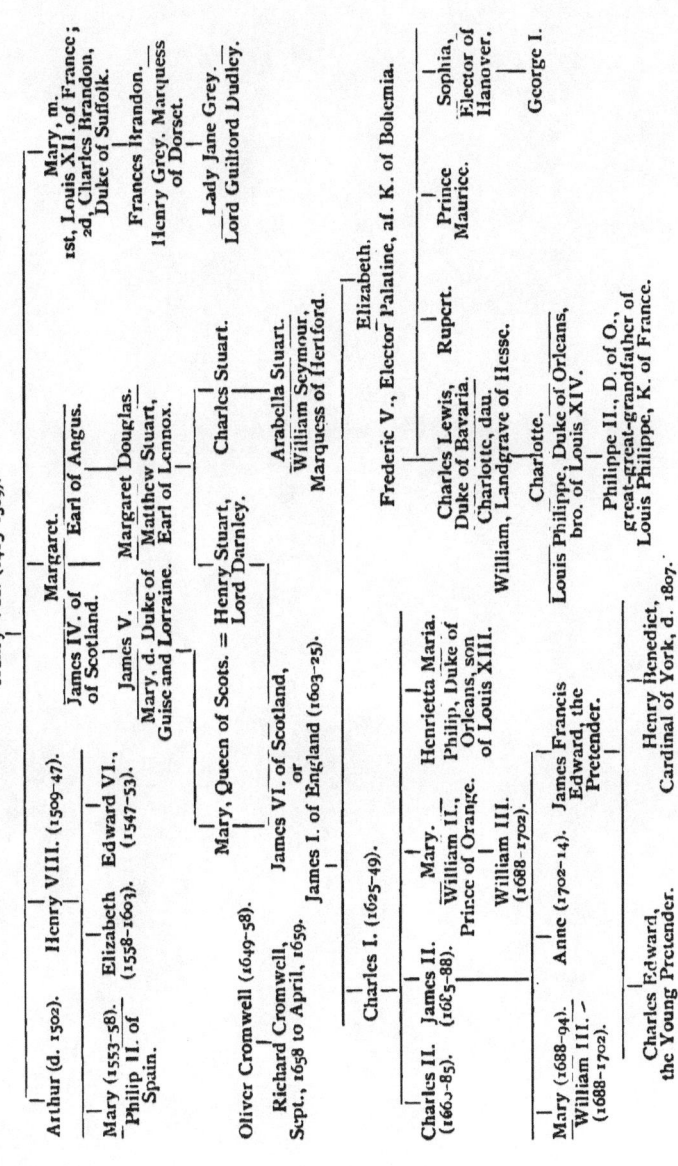

Henry VII. (1485-1509).

ENGLISH GENEALOGY—NO. 5.—THE HOUSE OF BRUNSWICK.

George I. (1714-27).

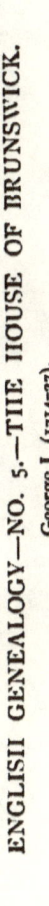

George II. (1727-60).

Sophia.
Frederick William III., K. of Prussia.

Frederick the Great.

Frederick. (d. 1751).

William Augustus, Duke of Cumberland.

Caroline Matilda.
Christian VII., K. of Denmark.

Frederick, K. of D. (1808-39).

Augusta.
Charles William, Duke of Brunswick Wolfenbuttel.

Henry Frederick, Duke of Cumberland.

William Henry, Duke of Gloucester.

Edward Augustus, Duke of Kent.

Caroline.
George IV.

Charlotte.
Duke of Wurtemberg.

Frederick William, D. of B., fell at Quatre Bras (see Byron's Waterloo).

Edward, Duke of Kent.
Victoria (1837).

William IV. (1830-37), Duke of Clarence.

Charles Augustus.
Frederica, dau. William, Prince of Orange.

Adolphus Frederick, Duke of Cambridge.

Augustus Frederick, Duke of Sussex.

Ernest, Duke of Cumberland, af. K. of Hanover.
George IV. K. of H. (d. 1878).

George IV. (1820-30).

Frederick, Duke of York and Albany.

Charlotte, Princess of Wales. (d. 1817).

Victoria. Albert Edward. Alice. Alfred. Helena. Louise. Arthur. Leopold. Beatrice.

THE SAXON LINE.

Cerdic, the ancestor of the kings of England of the Saxon line and the ninth in descent from Woden, founded the kingdom of Wessex 519. From his son Cynric, King of Wessex, is descended,—Egbert, son of Ealhmund, King of Kent, who, previously to his advent to the throne, held a command in the army of Charlemagne. In 800, he was called to assume the government of Wessex, and he subsequently succeeded in bringing all the kingdoms of the Heptarchy under his sway.

Egbert married Redburga.

Issue.—Ethelwolf; Athelstan, who had Kent and Essex; Editha.

Ethelwolf married, first, Osburga, daughter of Oslake, Great Butler of England; secondly, Judith, daughter Charles the Bald, King of France.

Ethelbald married his father's widow, Judith.

Alfred married Elswitha, daughter of Ethelred the Great, Ealdorman of Mercia.

Issue.—Edward the Elder; Ethelward; Ethelfleda; Ethelgiva; Alfritha, who married Baldwin, Count of Flanders, and was great-great-great-grandmother of Baldwin V., Count of Flanders, whose daughter Matilda married William the Conqueror.

Edward the Elder married, first, Egwina, daughter of a neat-herd; their children were Athelstan and Editha; secondly, Elfreda, daughter of Earl Ethelhelm; her daughter Egwina married Charles the Simple, King of France, and was by him mother of Giselle, first wife of the Norman, Rollo. Another daughter, Ethelda, married Hugh the Great, Count of Paris: Editha married the Emperor Otto I. The third

3

wife of Edward the Elder was Edgiva, daughter of Earl Sigelline of Kent. They had three sons : Edmund, who succeeded his brother Athelstan ; Edred, and Elfred, died young ; and two daughters, Edgiva and Thyra.

Athelstan, first monarch of England. At the age of thirty, by the splendid victory of Brunanburgh, he crushed his enemies and achieved the sovereignty of the whole island.

Edmund married, first, Elgiva ; secondly, Ethelfleda. By the former he had Edwy and Edgar.

Edwy married Elgiva, of the blood royal.

Edgar married, first, Elfleda, daughter of Ordman, a nobleman of East Anglia, by whom he had a son, Edward, his successor ; secondly, Elfrida, daughter of Ordgar, Earl of Devon, by whom he had a son, Ethelred.

Ethelred II. married, first, Elgiva, daughter of Thored, an English earl. Edmund, their son, succeeded, and Edwy was slain by the order of Canute. Secondly, Emma, called for her beauty, "The Pearl of Normandy," daughter of Richard I., Duke of Normandy. By her (who married, secondly, King Canute) he had Alfred, slain by Earl Godwin ; Edward the Confessor, who married Editha, daughter of Earl Godwin. Edward died without issue, and was the last Saxon king of the ancient blood royal of Cerdic.

Edmund Ironside married Algita, widow of Segeferth, a Danish Thane. His son, Edmund, married Agatha, daughter of Solomon, King of Hungary, who protected and educated him ; Edward married Agatha, daughter of Henry II., Emperor of Germany. Their children were, Edgar Atheling, who married Margaret, sister of Malcolm III., King of Scotland ; Margaret (married Malcolm III.); Christiana.

Godwin, Earl of Kent, d. 1053, married Githa, granddaughter of Harold Blatant, father of Sweyn.

Issue.—Editha, married Edward the Confessor ; Harold, married Agatha, daughter of Earl of Mercia ; Tosti, Earl of Northumberland, married Judith, daughter of Baldwin IV., Count of Flanders.

NORMAN LINE.

Rollo the Dane (died 931) married, first, Poppa, daughter of Berengarius, Count of Bayeux ; secondly, Gisela, daughter of Charles the Simple. By the former he had William, surnamed Longa-Spartha, Duke of Normandy, who married Adela, daughter of Hubert, Count of Senlis, and left a son and successor, Richard I., Duke of Normandy, who married Gunilda, a Danish lady. Their son Richard succeeded ; their daughter Emma married, first, Ethelred, King of England ; secondly, Canute the Great.

Richard II., Duke of Normandy, married Judith, daughter of the Duke of Brittany. His daughter Eleanor married Baldwin IV., Count of Flanders ; their son was Baldwin V., Count of Flanders ; who married Adela, daughter of Robert, King of France, son of Hugh Capet, and whose daughter Matilda married William, Duke of Normandy.

Duke Richard married, secondly, Eslrith, sister of Canute the Dane. He died 1026 and was succeeded by his eldest son, Richard III., Duke of Normandy, who was succeeded by his brother, Robert le Diable. The latter had a son, William, by Arlotta, the daughter of an officer in his household. Before his departure to the Crusades, he prevailed on an Assembly of the Barons to acknowledge him as heir to the Duchy.

William the Conqueror, born 1025, married Matilda, daughter of Baldwin V., Count of Flanders.

Issue.—Robert Courthose, who succeeded to the Duchy of Normandy; Richard, killed by a stag in the New Forest; William Rufus; Henry Beauclerc; Cecilia; Constance, married Duke of Brittany; Alice; Adela, married Stephen, Count of Blois; Agatha; Gundred.

William II., Rufus, born 1056, was not married.

Henry I., born 1070, married, first, Matilda, daughter of Malcolm III. of Scotland; secondly, Adelais, daughter of Godfrey, Duke of Louvaine, by whom he had no issue.

Stephen, born 1104, married Matilda, daughter of Eustace, Count of Boulogne.

Issue.—Eustace, Count of Boulogne, who married Constance, daughter of Louis VI., of France, and died before his father; William, Count of Boulogne, and other children, none of whom survived him.

Henry II., Curt, or Shortmantle, born 1133, married Eleanor, the divorced Queen of Louis VII. of France. Issue.— William, died an infant; Henry married Margaret, daughter of Louis VII. of France, and died before his father; Geoffrey married Constance, daughter of Conan le Petit, Earl of Richmond and Duke of Brittany (he was killed at a tournament); Matilda married Henry the Lion, Duke of Saxony, and became the ancestress of George I.; Eleanor married Alphonso VIII., King of Castile, and was mother of Blanche, Queen of Louis VIII. of France; Joan married, first, William II., King of Sicily; secondly Raymond, Count of Toulouse.

Richard I., Cœur de Lion, born 1157, married at Cyprus, Berengaria, daughter of Sancho the Wise, King of Navarre. Richard was made King of Cyprus and Jerusalem.

John, Lackland, born 1166, married, first, Isabella, daughter of William, Earl of Gloucester (was divorced on the ground of consanguinity); secondly, Isabella, daughter of Aymer Taillefer, Count of Angoulême. Their children were : Joan, married Alexander II., King of Scotland ; Eleanor, married, first, William, Earl of Pembroke; secondly, Simon Montfort, Earl of Leicester ; Isabella, married Frederick II., Emperor of Germany.

Henry III., Winchester, born 1206, married Eleanor, daughter of Raymond Berenger, Count of Provence (her sister Margaret married St. Louis, King of France). His daughter Margaret married Alexander III. of Scotland ; Beatrice married John, Duke of Brittany.

Edward I., Longshanks, born 1239, married, first, Eleanor, daughter of Ferdinand III. of Castile; secondly, Margaret, daughter of Philip III. of France. The children of his first wife were : Henry, died young; Alphonso; Edward II.; Eleanor, married, first, Alphonso, King of Aragon ; secondly, Comte de Bar in France (by the latter she was mother of Lady Eleanor, who married Llewelyn ap Owen, Lord of South Wales, and who became grandmother of Margaret, married to Meredith ap Tudor ; their son was Owen Tudor, grandfather of Henry VII.). Margaret married John, Duke of Brabant ; Joan married Gilbert de Clare, Earl of Gloucester and Hereford ; Elizabeth married, first, John, Earl of Holland and Zealand ; secondly, Humphrey de Bohun, Earl of Hereford and Essex.

By his second wife Edward had Thomas Brotherton, Earl of Norfolk, and first Earl Marshal of England, and Edmund of Woodstock, Earl of Kent.

Edward II., of Woodstock, Earl of Norfolk and Kent, sur-

named Caernarvon, born 1284, married Isabel, daughter
of Philip IV. of France. His daughter, Jane, married David
II. of Scotland; Eleanor married the Count de Gueldres.

Edward III., Windsor, born 1312, married Philippa, daughter of William of Hainault and Holland (Jane, the mother of
Philippa, was great-granddaughter of Louis IX. of France).
Isabelle, daughter of Edward and Philippa, married the
Earl of Bedford; Joan of the Tower was contracted in marriage with Alphonso, King of Castile, but died of the plague,
before the solemnization; Mary married the Duke of Brittany; Margaret married the Earl of Pembroke.

Edward, the Black Prince, born 1330, married Joan, the
Fair Maid of Kent.
Issue.—Edward of Angoulême, who died young, and
Richard.

Richard II., born 1366, married, first, Anne of Bohemia,
daughter of Emperor Charles IV.; secondly, Eleanor Isabelle,
daughter of Charles VI. of France. No children.

Lionel, Duke of Clarence, married, first, Elizabeth de
Burgh, great-granddaughter of Edmund Crouchback; sec-
ondly, Violante, daughter of Galeasius, Duke of Milan. Lionel
died in Piedmont 1398.
By his first wife he had Philippa, who married Edmund
Mortimer, Earl of March.

Roger Mortimer, son of Philippa and Edmund Mortimer,
was declared heir-apparent to the crown 1385, but was killed
in Ireland 1398. Richard II., previous to his last voyage to
Ireland, declared Edmund Mortimer heir-apparent. He was
trusted and employed by Henry V. during his reign, and died

of the plague at his castle at Trim, in Ireland, 1424, being only 32 years old.

Elizabeth, daughter of Philippa and Edmund Mortimer, married Henry Percy, Hotspur.

Roger Mortimer married Eleanora, daughter of Thomas, Earl of Kent.

Edmund Mortimer married Anne, daughter of Edmund, or fifth Earl of Stafford.

John Plantagenet, of Gaunt (born 1340, died 1399); married, first, Blanche of Lancaster; secondly, Constance of Castile, daughter of Pedro the Cruel; thirdly, Catherine Swynford, sister of Chaucer. He assumed in right of Constance, his second wife, the title of Castile and Leon. He was also Duke of Lancaster, Earl of Richmond, Derby, Lincoln and Leicester. He abandoned his claim to the throne of Castile, in consideration of a large sum of money and the marriage of his daughter by Constance, Katherine, to Henry, Prince of Asturias, afterwards Henry III., King of Castile and Leon.

By his first wife John had Henry; Elizabeth, who married John Holland, Duke of Exeter; Philippa, married John, King of Portugal (from this marriage descended Mary Isabelle, Queen of Spain; Ferdinand, King of Naples; Pedro, Emperor of the Brazils; Frederick Augustus, King of Saxony; the Emperor of Austria and the Grand Duke of Tuscany).

The children of John and Catherine were: John de Beaufort, first Earl of Somerset, who married Margaret, daughter of Thomas Holland, Earl of Kent; Henry, Bishop of Lincoln and Winchester; Thomas, Duke of Exeter; Joan, who married Ralph, Earl of Westmoreland (their grandson was Warwick, the King-Maker).

The children of John Beaufort and Margaret were : Henry Beaufort, second Earl of Somerset ; John Beaufort, third Earl of Somerset, who married Margaret, daughter of Sir John Beauchamp, and whose daughter was Margaret, who married Edmund Tudor ; Edmund, fourth Earl of Somerset, married Lady Alianor Beauchamp, co-heiress with Ralph, Earl of Westmoreland ; Joan married James I., King of Scotland; Margaret married Thomas, Earl of Devon.

Edmund Plantagenet, Duke of York, surnamed Langley, from the place of his birth, was created by his father, Earl of Cambridge, and by his nephew, Richard II., Duke of York. He married, first, Isabel, daughter of Pedro the Cruel, King of Castile and Leon, by whom he had : Edward, his successor in the Dukedom of York, created by Richard II. Duke of Aumerle (he fell at Agincourt) ; Richard of Conisburgh, who succeeded to the Earldom of Cambridge, and was beheaded at Southampton, 1415, for conspiring against Henry IV., when the Earldom of Cambridge became forfeited. He married Anne, sister of Edmund Mortimer, Earl of March, by whom he had : Richard, who succeeded his uncle as Duke of York, and Isabel, who married Henry Bouchier, Earl of Essex. Richard was restored to the Earldom of Cambridge and allowed to inherit as third Duke of York. He married Cicely, daughter of Ralph Nevil, Earl of Westmoreland.

Their children were : Edward IV.; Edmund, Earl of Rutland, murdered at the age of 12, by Lord Clifford, after the Battle of Wakefield ; George, Duke of Clarence, married Isabelle, daughter of Earl of Warwick ; Anne ; Margaret, married Charles the Bold, Duke of Burgundy, and became the patron of Caxton and the unrelenting foe of Henry VII.; Richard III.; Elizabeth, married John de la Pole, Duke of Suffolk. Their son, the Earl of Lincoln, was declared by Richard III. his successor, after the death of his own son.

Henry IV., Bolingbroke, born 1367. He was created Earl of Hereford, after his marriage with Mary, daughter of Humphrey, last Earl of Hereford. When he came to the throne, his great inheritance with the Dukedom of Lancaster and the Earldoms of Hereford, Derby, Lincoln and Leicester, merged in the crown. He married, secondly, Isabella Joan, daughter of Charles the Bad, King of Navarre, and widow of John V., Duke of Bretagne. Issue, by his first wife only,— Henry; Thomas, Duke of Clarence; Humphrey, Duke of Gloucester; John, Duke of Bedford; Blanche; Philippa.

His son, John, Duke of Bedford, Regent of France, married, first, Anne, daughter of John, Duke of Burgundy; secondly, Jacqueline, daughter of Peter of Luxemburgh.

Her daughter, by her second husband, Sir Richard Wydeville was Elizabeth, who married Edward IV.

Henry's daughter, Blanche, married, first, Duke of Bavaria; secondly, King of Aragon; thirdly, Duke de Baar. His daughter, Philippa, married Eric XIII., King of Denmark.

Henry V., Monmouth, born 1388 married Catherine, daughter of Charles VI., of France.

Henry VI., Windsor, born 1421, was crowned King of England and France, in 1429 at Westminster, and at Paris in 1430. His father-in-law, René, Duke of Anjou, was titular King of Sicily, Naples, and Jerusalem, and was great-grandson of John, King of France.

Issue.—Edward, killed by Richard, Duke of Gloucester.

Edward IV., born 1441, married Lady Elizabeth Grey, daughter of Sir Richard Wydeville.

Issue.—Edward V. (born 1470, murdered 1483), reigned two months and twelve days of the year 1483. Although proclaimed king a few days after his father's death, he was never crowned ; Richard, Duke of York, born 1472 ; Elizabeth married Henry VII.; George, Duke of Bedford, died young ; Cicely ; Anne ; Bridget ; Mary ; Catherine.

Richard III., Crookback, born 1450, married Anne Neville, daughter of Earl of Warwick, and widow of Edward, son of Henry VI.

Issue.—Edward ; died 1484.

Henry VII., Tudor, born 1455; married Elizabeth, daughter of Edward IV.

His son, Arthur, married Catherine, daughter of Ferdinand of Aragon, and died 1502.

Henry VIII., born 1491; married: first (1509), Catherine of Aragon, widow of his brother, Arthur ; secondly (1532), Anne, daughter of Sir Thomas Boleyn ; thirdly (1536), Jane Seymour, daughter of Sir John Seymour ; fourthly (January, 1539), Anne, daughter of John, Duke of Cleves, was divorced in July of the same year ; fifthly (August, 1540), Katherine, daughter of Sir Edmund Howard and own cousin of Anne Boleyn, she was beheaded, February, 1542 ; sixthly (1543), Katherine, daughter of Sir Thomas Parr, and relict of the Hon. Edward Borough and of John Neville, Lord Latimer.

By his first wife he had Mary, and three sons and a daughter, who died in infancy ; by Anne Boleyn, he had Elizabeth ; and by Jane Seymour, Edward.

Anne of Cleves, died 1557, and was buried in Westminster Abbey.

Edward VI., born 1537. He was not married.

Mary I., born 1516 ; married, 1554, Philip II., son of Charles V., Emperor of Germany. Their titles were : Philip and Mary by the Grace of God, King and Queen of England and France, Naples, Jerusalem and Ireland, Defenders of the Faith, Princes of Spain and Sicily, Archdukes of Austria, Duke of Milan, Burgundy and Brabant, etc.

Elizabeh, born 1533, was not married.

James I., born 1566, married Anne, daughter of Frederick II. of Denmark.
Issue.—Henry, died 1612 ; Charles I. ; Robert of Carrick ; Margaret ; Mary ; Sophia, died young.

Charles I., born 1600 ; married Henrietta Maria, daughter of Henry IV. of France.
His son, Henry, Duke of Gloucester, died 1660. Elizabeth died of grief, a prisoner in Carrisbrook Castle, aged 15.

Oliver Cromwell, born 1599, married Elizabeth, daughter of Sir J. Bouchier of Essex.
Issue.—Richard ; Henry ; and four daughters.

Charles II., born 1630, married the Infanta Catherine, daughter of John IV., of Portugal, by whom he had no issue.

James II., born 1663, married, first, Anne, eldest daughter of Edward Hyde, Earl of Clarendon ; secondly, Mary Beatrice D'Este, daughter of Alphonso III., Duke of Modena. By his first wife, he had Mary and Anne ; Charles ; James ; Charles ; Edgar ; Henrietta ; and Catherine, who died young. By his second wife, he had James Francis Edward, born 1688 (the Chevalier St. George, or The Pretender), who married Mary, daughter of Prince James Sobieski (son of John, King of Poland).
Their children were : Charles Edward (died 1788), married Louisa Maximiliana, Princess Stohlberg ; Henry Benedict, Cardinal York (died 1807); Charles ; Catherine ; Isabel ; Elizabeth ; Charlotte (died young) ; Louise, died unmarried.

William III., the posthumous son of William, Prince of Orange, by Mary, eldest daughter of Charles I.

The period between December 11, 1688, and February 13, 1689, when William and Mary commenced their reign, was called " The Interregnum."

They had no children.

Anne, second daughter of James II., born 1665, married Prince George of Denmark, second son of Frederick III. He was not allowed to assume the title of king, but was styled " His Highness, Prince George." All their seventeen children died in infancy, except William, who lived to be eleven years old.

George I., Guelph, Elector of Hanover and Duke of Bruns-wick Luneburgh, born 1660, was the eldest son of Ernest Augustus, Elector of Hanover, by Sophia, granddaughter of James I. He married, 1682, his cousin, the Princess Sophia Dorothea, daughter of George William, Duke of Zelle, and was divorced, 1694.

George II., born 1683, married Wilhelmina Carolina, daughter of John Frederick, Margrave of Brandenburgh-Anspach. Issue.—Anne, married William, Prince of Orange ; Mary married Frederick, Landgrave of Hesse-Cassel ; Louisa married Frederick V., King of Denmark ; Amelia ; Elizabeth.

His eldest son Frederick (died 1751) married Augusta, daughter of Frederick II., Duke of Saxe-Gotha.

George III., born 1738, married Charlotte Sophia, Princess of Mecklenburg Strelitz. His daughter Charlotte married the King of Wurtemburg ; Edward, Duke of Kent, married Princess Victoria of Leiningen, sister of Leopold, husband of

Queen Charlotte. Ernest married Frederica, daughter of the Duke of Mecklenburg Strelitz ; Elizabeth married the Landgrave of Hesse-Homburg ; Mary married her cousin, the Duke of Gloucester ; Augusta ; Sophia ; Octavius ; Alfred ; Amelia.

George IV., born 1762, married Caroline of Brunswick (died 1821).

Their daughter Charlotte (died 1817) married Prince Leopold of Saxe-Coburg, afterwards King of Belgium.

William IV., married Adelaide, daughter of the Duke of Saxe-Meiningen.

Issue.—Two daughters who died in infancy.

William, as Prince, was Lord High Admiral of England.

Victoria Alexandrina, Queen of the United Kingdom of Great Britain and Ireland, and of its Colonies and Dependencies in Europe, Asia, Africa, America and Oceanica, Empress of India, Defender of the Faith, was the only daughter of Edward, Duke of Kent. She was born May 24, 1819, raised to the throne June 20, 1837, crowned June 28, 1838, and married February 10, 1840, to her cousin, Francis Albert, Duke of Saxony and Prince of Saxe-Coburg and Gotha (born August 26, 1819, died December 14, 1861).

Issue.—1. Victoria Adelaide Mary Louise, Princess Royal, born 1840 ; married, 1858, Prince Frederick William of Prussia, only son of William Louis, Emperor of Germany and King of Prussia.

2. Albert Edward, Prince of Wales, Duke of Saxony, of Cornwall and Rothesay, Earl of Chester, Carrick and Dublin, Baron of Renfrew and Lord of the Isles, Prince of Saxe-Coburg and Gotha, Great Steward of Scotland, born November 9, 1841, married, March 10, 1863, Princess Alexandra,

daughter of Christian IX., of Denmark (born December 1, 1844).

3. Alice Maud Mary, born 1843, married Prince Charles Louis (since Grand Duke) of Hesse Darmstadt, died 1878.

4. Alfred Ernest, Duke of Edinburgh, born 1844, married, 1874, the Arch-Duchess Marie Alexandrovna, only daughter of Alexander II., Emperor of Russia.

5. Helena Augusta Victoria, born 1846, married Prince Christian of Schleswig-Holstein.

6. Louise Carolina Alberta, born 1848, married, 1871, John Douglas Sutherland Campbell, Marquis of Lorne, late Governor-General of the Dominion of Canada, eldest son of the Duke of Argyll.

7. Arthur William Patrick Albert, born 1850, Duke of Connaught and Strathearn, Earl of Sussex, married, 1879, the Princess Louise Margaret, third daughter of His Royal Highness Prince Frederick Charles of Prussia.

8. Leopold George Duncan Albert, born 1853, Baron Arklow, Earl of Clarence and Duke of Albany, married Princess Hélène of Waldeck, daughter of His Serene Highness George Victor, reigning Prince of Waldeck and Pyrmont, died 1884.

9. Beatrice Mary Victoria Feodore, born 1857, married, July, 1885, Prince Henry of Battenberg. His elder brother married the daughter of Princess Alice.

Children of Victoria and Frederick William :
Frederick William Victor Albert, born 1859; married, 1881,

the Princess Augusta Victoria, eldest daughter of the Grand
Duke of Schleswig-Holstein.
Albert William Henry, born 1862.

Francis Frederick Sigismund, born 1864, died 1866,
Joachim Frederick Ernest Waldemar, born 1868, died 1879,
Victoria Elizabeth Augusta Charlotte, born 1860; married,
1878, Bernard, Hereditary Prince of Saxe-Meiningen, and has
issue Feodora Victoria, born 1879,
Frederika Amelia Wilhelmina Victoria, born 1866,
Sophie Dorothea Ulrique Alice, born 1870,
Margaretta Beatrice Feodore, born 1872.

Children of Albert Edward:
Albert Victor Christian Edward, born 1864,
George Frederick Ernest Albert, born 1865,
Louise Victoria Alexandra Dagmar, born 1867,
Victoria Alexandra Olga Marie, born 1868,
Maud Charlotte Marie Victoria, born 1869,
Alexander John Charles Albert, born 1871.

Children of Alice:
Ernest Louis Christian Albert William, Hereditary Grand
Duke of Hesse, born 1868,
Friedrich Wilhelm August Victor Leopold Ludwig, accident-
ally killed 1873,
Victoria Alberta Elizabeth Matilda Mary, born 1863,
Elizabeth Alexandrina Louise Alice, born 1864,
Irene Mary Louise Anna, born 1866,
Victoria Alice Helene Louise Beatrice, born 1872,
Marie Victoria Feodore Leopoldine, born 1874, died 1878.

Children of Alfred:
Alfred Alexander William Ernest Albert, born 1874,
Marie Alexandra Victoria, born 1875,

Victoria Melita, born 1877,
Alexandrina Louise Olga Victoria, born 1878.

Children of Helena :
Christian Victor Albert Ludwig Ernest, born 1867,
Albert John Christian Frederick Alfred George, born 1869,
Frederick Christian Augustus Leopold Edward Harold,
born 1876, died 1876,
Victoria Louise Sophie Augusta Amelia Helena, born 1870,
Franziska Josepha Louise Augusta Marie Christiana Helena,
born 1872.

Daughter of Leopold, Alice Marie Victoria Augusta Pauline,
born 1883.